Patsy    Roscoe    P.B. Bear    Milly

Bob    Hilda    Dermott    Dixie    Russell    Florrie

FAMILY LEARNING

**Managing Art Editor** Chris Fraser  **Managing Editor** Bridget Gibbs  **Senior Designer** Claire Jones
**Project Editor** Natascha Biebow  **Designer** Peter Fickling
**DTP Design** Kim Browne  **Production** Katy Holmes  **Photography** Dave King

First published in Great Britain in 1998

Visit us on the World Wide Web at: http://www.dk.com

Copyright © 1998 Dorling Kindersley Limited, London

4 6 8 10 9 7 5

A CIP catalogue record for this book is available from the British Library.

ISBN 0 7513 7150 5

Reproduced in Italy by G.R.B. Editrice, Verona    Printed and bound in Italy by L.E.G.O.

**Acknowledgments**
Dorling Kindersley would like to thank the following manufacturers for permission to photograph copyright material:
Ty Inc. for "Toffee" the dog and "Freddie" the frog; Folkmanis, Inc. for the toy hen puppet.

Dorling Kindersley would also like to thank Maggie Haden, Richard Blakey, Barbara Owen,
Vera Jones, and Dave King for their help with props and set design.

Can you find me
in each scene?

# P.B. BEAR

# The Pyjama Party

### Lee Davis

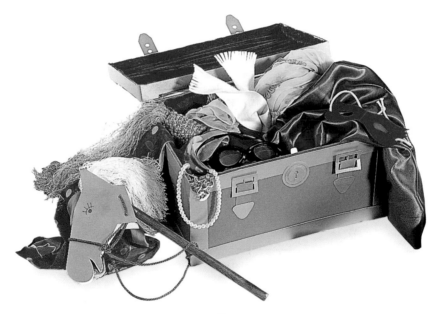

FAMILY LEARNING

One day, P.B. Bear and his friends were playing dressing up at his house. "Vroom, vroom," zoomed Hilda. "Treasure ahoy!" shouted Dermott. "Charge!" Roscoe galloped on his horse. "Lights, camera, action!" sang Florrie, flicking her golden wig in the air. "Look at me. I'm a superbear!" said P.B. Bear, racing around the sitting room.

Suddenly P.B. Bear ran past the clock on the mantlepiece. "Oh, no!" he cried, holding it up. "We were having so much fun we didn't notice how late it is!"

The friends all ran to the window and looked out.

"It's dark outside," said Roscoe.
"And I'm afraid of the dark."
"It's raining," said Hilda. "I hate getting wet."
"I hear thunder," said Dermott.
"I'm scared of loud noises."
"What are we going to do?" asked Florrie.
"I know," said P.B. Bear. "You can all spend
the night at my house. That way nobody
will have to go out in the dark, get wet,
or be alone with the thunder."
"Yes, please!" cried the friends.

"What about pyjamas?" asked Roscoe.

"I'm the only one who has to wear pyjamas," said P.B., "because I'm Pyjama Bedtime Bear. Everyone else can stay in their dressing-up clothes."

"Yeah!" said Roscoe. "I can be a knight all night long!"

P.B. Bear put on his pyjamas, then added his mask, his belt, and his cape. "Look, everyone, Super Pyjama Bedtime Bear is ready for bed."

"But where are we going to sleep?" asked Hilda.

"I don't think there is enough room in your bed for all of us," said Florrie.

"No," said Dermott, shaking his head.

"Don't worry," said P.B. "I'll find a special place for each of you."

P.B. Bear looked around his room. "Roscoe, you can borrow my sleeping bag, and sleep right next to my bed." "And my horse can sleep right next to me!" said Roscoe. "Good idea," said P.B. Bear. "Here, take my torch. Then you won't be scared of the dark," said P.B. Bear. "Thanks, P.B.!" said Roscoe.

"What about me?" asked Hilda.

"Hmm," thought P.B. Bear. "You need a dry nest."

"You could sleep on the windowsill," suggested Florrie.

"Oh, no," said Hilda. "That's too close to the rain.
Vroom, vroom . . . I'll sleep here high up on
P.B.'s chest of drawers where I won't get wet."

"Where do you want to sleep, Florrie?" asked P.B. Bear.
"How about in this basket?"
"Oh, no," said Florrie.
"Actresses can't sleep
in *baskets*. I want to
sleep in a hammock."

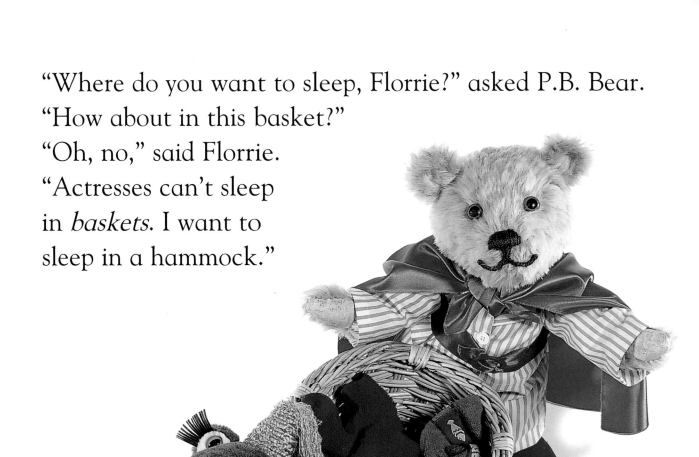

"We could use this scarf to make you one," said Hilda.
So she helped P.B. Bear and Florrie string up a
hammock between the bed and the chest of drawers.
Florrie hopped in. "Ahh," she said, "just right."
"What about Dermott?" asked P.B. Bear,
looking around his room. "Where could he sleep?"
"Oh," they all said at once. "Where is Dermott?"

The friends looked everywhere in P.B. Bear's room. They looked on top of the bookshelf, in the toy box, under the duvet, behind the bedside table . . .

. . . until at last P.B. Bear cried, "Here he is!
He's hiding from the thunder!"

Dermott opened one eye, grunted, and rolled over.
"Shhh!" whispered the friends. "Time for bed."

So they all snuggled down to
sleep in their special beds.
"Good night!" called P.B. Bear.
"Good night, P.B.,"
whispered his friends.